FIND YOUR WAY TO

JURASSIC PARK™

FIND YOUR WAY TO

JURASSIC PARK™

By
Dinah Sawyer

GROSSET & DUNLAP • NEW YORK

Start by Reading This

Are you ready to take a trip to Jurassic Park and have some amazing adventures?

Begin reading on page 1. Keep reading until you come to a page where you are asked to make a choice. Decide what you want to do, and then turn to that page. Keep reading and making choices until you come to THE END. Now one adventure is over. But there are plenty of others in this book. Go back to where you started. A new adventure is always about to begin!

School's out for vacation! Yippee!

As you throw your books onto the kitchen counter, you see a set of plane tickets. The writing on the ticket envelope says HAWAII!! Too cool! You've always dreamed of catching a big wave, and now's your chance!

Your parents come into the kitchen and see you looking at the tickets.

"Isn't it thrilling?" your mother asks.

"Great!" you say.

Your father looks surprised. "It's really nice of you to be so happy for your mother and me, going off on our second honeymoon." He gives Mom a little hug.

You say, "Huh?"

Then the truth comes out. Your parents bought two tickets to Hawaii. The third ticket—*your* ticket—is to St. Louis, where Gramma Dottie lives in an apartment. While your parents are taking hula lessons and pigging out at luaus, you'll be spending six weeks sleeping on Gramma Dottie's lumpy couch.

"Gramma lives just two blocks from a library," says your mom on the way to the airport.

"And if you behave yourself," your father adds, "Gramma will take you up in the Arch, where you can see all the way to Illinois."

Go to page 2.

On the plane, the flight attendant tries to pin a pair of gold plastic junior pilot wings on your T-shirt that say, "I'm big enough to fly all by myself!" You say, "Thanks—but no thanks."

After they serve what they call lunch (and what you call disgusting!) they start the in-flight movie. As the title rolls up on the screen, you see that the movie's called *The Day the Dinosaurs Took Over.*

If you want to catch the movie, turn to page **7.**

If you'd rather catch a few z's, turn to page **13.**

"Wait!" you cry jumping out of the jeep and running after Mr. Gennaro. "Wait for me!"

But Mr. Gennaro is only interested in one thing—saving himself. He dashes into the little wooden building, slamming the door behind him.

You bang on the door! You look over your shoulder. The T-rex is thundering toward you. Yikes! You sprint away! You run down the road. As you're running, you realize you don't hear thundering footsteps. You turn just in time to see T-rex kick the shed to bits!

There's Mr. Gennaro, cowering in the corner. But not for long. T-rex picks the lawyer up in its teeth, tosses him into the air, and . . . *GULP!*

Looks like for Mr. Gennaro, this is . . .

THE END

But what about you? Quick! Look at page 4!

You keep running. Just down the road you see another jeep. It's on the road, not on a track, and Mr. Muldoon is at the wheel.

"Jump in!" cries Mr. Muldoon.

You don't have to be asked twice.

Mr. Muldoon floors it and drives you back to the Visitors' Center, just in time for you to catch the next helicopter off the island. From a safe distance of 500 feet in the air, you look down. Boy, that Isla Nublar was one scary place! Boy, are you glad to be out of there! Boy, are you glad that this story has finally come to . . .

THE END

"I don't feel so good," you say.

"Hmmm," says Dr. Sattler. "I gave the Trike an injection to protect her from poison berries—just in case. Maybe I should give you one, too."

The only problem is that the needle she's holding is about the size of a broomstick.

"Hey, I feel better now!" you tell Dr. Sattler.

The two of you walk back to the spot where you bumped into each other.

"Look!" you cry, pointing up. "A rope's dangling down from that helicopter. Help has arrived!"

You start climbing, but Dr. Sattler says, "I drove in here, and I'm driving out."

She starts walking toward her jeep as the helicopter lifts you up into the air. You can see green jungle, blue ocean, and . . . brown animals! They're running fast—at cheetah-speed, maybe—toward Dr. Sattler. Even from fifty feet in the air, you can see their sharp teeth! Oh, no! It's those dinosaurs Tim was talking about! Raptors! You've got to warn Dr. Sattler! You yell! You scream! But you're too far up in the air! She can't hear you! What are you going to do?

If you let go of the rope, turn to page 46.

If you keep holding on to the rope, turn to page 36.

"But Gramma Dottie!" you exclaim as she hurries you toward the gate. "Mom and Dad think . . . I mean, I'm supposed to stay here with . . ."

"Shhhh!" Gramma Dottie gives you a look. "Here's your passport," she whispers, handing it to you. "This isn't exactly a spur-of-the-moment thing. You are going to have the time of your life!"

"I am?" you say as you reach the gate and she hands you a ticket.

"You are!" she says, waving good-bye. "And don't be surprised," she calls after you, "if you run into some-one you know!"

Go to page **19.**

You tune your headphones to the movie channel, lean your seat back, and get ready to enjoy the show.

But suddenly you realize that you've seen *The Day the Dinosaurs Took Over!* When you were in kindergarten, one of your friends who was really into dinosaurs rented it for his birthday party—and you watched it—FOUR times!

Oh, well, you're stuck now. All you can do is keep watching one more time until . . .

THE END

Mr. Hammond rustles you all out of the Visitors' Center to where three jeeps are parked. You get into one of them with Tim, Dr. Grant, and the nervous-looking lawyer, Mr. Gennaro.

"Where's the driver?" asks Mr. Gennaro, as your jeep takes off with a jerk.

"These jeeps run on electrified rails!" Mr. Hammond shouts. "Enjoy the tour! Enjoy the park!"

Your jeep is in the lead. It starts down the road, heading right for a huge iron gate. Just as it seems as if you are going to crash into it, the gate swings open.

Now a computer screen flashes on the dashboard. It shows you the area of the park that you are passing. A deep voice says, "Welcome to Jurassic Park!"

"Jurassic?" you say, a bad feeling coming over you. "What kind of park is this, anyway?"

Go to page **9**.

Dr. Grant turns around and you think he's about to tell you what kind of park it is when all of a sudden, off in the jungle to your left, you see a large, brownish animal nibbling the leaves off the trees—off the *tops* of the trees. Something tells you it isn't a giraffe!

Dr. Grant is leaning halfway out of the jeep as he tries to get a closer look at the beast. "It's a Brachiosaur!" he exclaims, and with that, he hops out of the jeep and starts running over to a thirty-five-foot-tall something that looks like a *dinosaur!*

"Wait! Dr. Grant!" Tim yells. "I'm coming with you!" He, too, jumps out of the jeep and races off into the jungle.

Turn to page 10.

You *know* that the Brachiosaur must be a big robot. But still, it sure looks real. No way are you getting out of the jeep. As a matter of fact, you wish you could make it turn around and go *back* to the Visitors' Center. But it just keeps gliding down the track farther into the jungle.

"They shouldn't have gotten out," scolds Mr. Gennaro. "No telling what might happen to them with real dinosaurs roaming around all over the place."

"Mr. Gennaro," you say, "what do you mean, *real*?"

The lawyer turns and gives you a funny look. "Didn't Hammond tell you?" he asks. "That dinosaur you just saw was as real as you and I are."

You say, "Huh?"

Mr. Gennaro waves his hands around as he tries to explain. "See, there were these prehistoric mosquitoes and Hammond got some scientists who . . ."

If you want to hear a lawyer explain DNA cloning, turn to page 18.

If you already understand exactly how DNA cloning works, you might as well quit school now and get a good-paying job.

If you just want to get on with this story, turn to page 11.

Your mind is spinning. Mr. Gennaro actually believes that the Brachiosaur was real!

As the jeep moves down the track, past a sign that says T-REX PADDOCK, you consider your position. Either you are alone in a jeep on an isolated island with a highly delusional person, or that dinosaur *was* real. And if the Brachiosaur was real, then . . . that forty-foot lizard running along on the other side of the fence— the one with teeth the size of bananas—the one that's got its yellow eyes right on *you*—then that T-rex is real, too!

Your heart is pounding like a drum, but you can't even hear it because the thunder of the T-rex's footsteps drowns it out. You grab on to the sleeve of Mr. Gennaro's safari suit.

But Mr. Gennaro shakes you off. "Relax," he says, scornfully. "Hammond told me that these fences are highly electrified. If that monster so much as brushes up against the metal, he'll be electrocuted."

Go to page 12.

The jeep rounds a curve in the road.

"Do you think we're slowing down?" you ask Mr. Gennaro as your jeep rolls to a stop.

The computer screen blinks and then goes blank. Everything is very quiet.

"Something's wrong," says Mr. Gennaro.

On the other side of the fence, the T-rex looks as if it's thinking the same thing as Mr. Gennaro. Reaching out one of its short forearms, T-rex touches the fence.

It's a highly-charged electric fence, right? When a T-rex touches it, you should hear the sound of a zillion bug zappers crackling in the air, right?

But you don't.

You don't hear anything. The fence isn't working.

Turn to page 22.

You push the call button and ask the flight attendant to bring you a blanket and a pillow. You try to sleep, but every time you open your eyes, even a little bit, you catch a glimpse of fake-looking giant lizards scampering across the screen. Oh, yawn. You really don't understand all the fuss about dinosaurs. It's not like anyone's ever really seen one. The whole idea of huge reptiles that stomped around on the earth about a zillion years ago seems pretty incredible.

But since you can't sleep, you decide you might as well watch the stupid movie. You put on the headphones, and in three seconds flat—zzzzzz. You're out. The next thing you know, the flight attendant is tapping you on the shoulder, and the plane is making its descent into the St. Louis International Airport.

Go to page **14.**

When you deplane, you pick out Gramma Dottie right away. She's the short woman in the bright purple jogging suit. When she sees you, she waves and calls, "Over here!"

As you walk toward Gramma, you notice two kids standing beside her. One is a boy with brown hair and a red-and-white-striped T-shirt. He's holding a thick book with—what else?—a dinosaur on the cover. If you had to guess, you'd say he was about nine. Next to him is a blonde girl in a paisley tank top and jeans. In one hand, she's holding a tiny computer. She looks about twelve.

"So, you made it!" Gramma Dottie says, giving you a hug. "Now, meet my friends. This is Alexis."

The girl gives you a little wave. "Call me Lex," she says.

"And this is Tim," says Gramma.

"Call me Tim," says Tim.

"Hi," you say.

Go to page 15.

"I've known Lex and Tim's grandfather, John Hammond, all my life," explains Gramma Dottie. "He lived next door to me when we were growing up. Oh, the times we had!" Gramma Dottie gets a far-off look in her eyes. Then she shakes her head. "Anyway," she goes on, "John's invited Lex and Tim to come and see him at a theme park he's building on an island off the coast of South America."

"Wow!" you say. "Are you here to catch your plane?" you ask.

"Yes," says Lex. She turns to Gramma Dottie. "Our flight leaves in thirty minutes, Mrs. Parker. We'd better go to the gate, don't you think?"

"You're right," says Gramma Dottie.

"Maybe I'd better go to the baggage claim and get my suitcase and meet you somewhere, Gramma," you suggest.

"Oh, that's not necessary," says Gramma Dottie, as she yanks you by the elbow. "I've arranged for your bags to be checked all the way through."

"Through?" you say. "Through to where?"

"To the island, silly," says Gramma Dottie. "You're going with Tim and Lex!"

If you'd rather stay in St. Louis with Gramma, turn to page 6.

If you're up for the trip to the island, turn to page 17.

Uh-oh. Poison control doesn't have any information on purple berries growing on plants that have been extinct for more than seven million years.

And by the time the ambulance arrives, you'll be extinct, too. Sad to say, as far as you're concerned, this story has come to . . .

THE END

Before you can say "Dilophosaurus"—not that *you* ever would say Dilophosaurus—you're sitting between Lex and Tim on a plane that's headed for . . . for . . . uh . . .

"Lex?" you say. "Where are we going exactly?"

"Our grandfather owns this island," Lex begins, turning off her handheld computer to save the batteries. "It's called Isla Nublar, and it's forty degrees latitude from the easternmost point of the southern continent."

Oh, now you know *exactly* where you're going!

"And," Lex continues, "he's turning the whole thing into a gigantic theme park."

"Grandpa says his park is going to be so amazing," adds Tim, "it'll make Disneyland look like a game of Candy Land."

"What's so great about it?" you ask.

Lex sighs. "The truth is we don't really know."

"Grandpa's kept it a big fat secret," says Tim.

Just as you're about to ask Tim and Lex some more questions, the lights dim and the in-flight movie begins.

"Oh, boy!" exclaims Tim. "My favorite movie! *The Day the Dinosaurs Took Over!*"

Here's another chance to catch that movie—turn to page 7.

If you'd rather pass, turn to page 27.

" . . . believed it stood to reason that if a mosquito bit a dinosaur and filled up on its blood, and then got stuck in some tree sap, which preserved it for millions of years . . . Are you with me?"

"I think so," you tell him.

"So," Mr. Gennaro goes on, "the scientists took blood from the prehistoric mosquitoes. They did it without a warrant, so the mosquitoes have a right to sue for improper search and seizure, but the mosquitoes have not exercised this right—or even expressed the desire to appear on *The People's Court*. Sure enough, the scientists extracted from the blood strands of the dinosaur's DNA, which are the building blocks of life, and if there were any missing segments in the DNA, they filled them in with frog DNA, also a highly illegal procedure, in which the frogs have every right to prosecute for invasion of DNA rights . . ."

Mr. Gennaro is going on and on and on. Pretty soon, you think he might *bore* you to death! When, oh when, is this guy ever going to come to . . .

THE END?

On the plane, Tim tells you and Lex all about these dinosaurs he thinks are amazing, Velociraptors.

"They're called Raptors, for short," Tim says. "They could run as fast as cheetahs—sixty miles an hour! They had razor-sharp teeth and were incredible jumpers."

With conversation like this, the trip whizzes by. Before you know it, you've landed and you're boarding a helicopter that will take you to Mr. Hammond's island. "Cool!" you exclaim as the chopper rises straight up into the air. A few minutes later, you catch a glimpse of an island looming out of the waves. Even though thick clouds cover much of it, you can tell the island has dense forests and steep cliffs. There's something strange and mysterious about the place.

Lex elbows you. "It looks sort of . . . prehistoric, doesn't it?" she whispers.

"I know what you mean," you say as the helicopter begins to drop straight down the face of a cliff. "It looks like it belongs to another time."

Go to page 20.

"Welcome to Jurassic Park!" says a white-haired man as you climb out of the helicopter. He hugs Lex and Tim, then they introduce you.

"Let's not waste any time," Mr. Hammond says, opening the door of a jeep. "Climb in and I'll show you the park!"

You all pile into the jeep and take off. The first thing Dr. Hammond points out is the large Visitors' Center. The building doesn't look quite finished yet. And are those *bars* on the windows? You whiz on down the road, past the Center. The island is very lush and green. But there sure are a lot of fences.

"There sure are a lot of fences," says Tim.

"Right you are!" said Mr. Hammond. "Fifty miles of them, and every inch is highly electrified."

"But why?" you ask. "Are there . . . wild animals in this park?"

"You could say that." Mr. Hammond chuckles.

You are just about to point out to Mr. Hammond that there's a good-sized hole in one of the fences when Lex says, "What are those strange trees, Grandpa? The ones with the big trunks."

Mr. Hammond just chuckles again but Tim cries out, "Dinosaurs!"

Go to page 21.

He's right! You see that the big tree trunks are really *legs!* You look up, up, up, and there's a dinosaur head!

Your head is starting to feel dizzy!

"It's a Brachiosaur!" cries Tim. "A real, live Brachiosaur!"

"Excellent identification!" exclaims Mr. Hammond.

"Shouldn't we keep . . . going?" you ask as the jeep comes to a stop. You notice that there isn't just *one* Brachiosaur—there's a whole *herd* of them!

"Relax," says Mr. Hammond. "They're herbivores. Just big, gentle plant-eaters." He hops out of the jeep. "Okay, who wants to pet a dinosaur?"

If you're feeling brave, turn to page 39.

If you'd just as soon pet a great white shark, turn to page 24.

The lawyer lunges into the driver's seat of the jeep and starts spinning the steering wheel like some little kid in a twenty-five-cent parking-lot ride. Nothing happens.

"This electrical system isn't working!" Mr. Gennaro cries. Beads of sweat are rolling down his face. "But . . . I'm sure Hammond will have it back on in no time."

But will it be *in* time? T-rex is shaking the fence! Shaking it, tearing it, ripping it to shreds!

With a scream of terror, Mr. Gennaro leaps from the jeep and runs into a small half-finished building by the side of the road.

The T-rex steps over what's left of the fence. It's heading straight for you. What are you going to do?

**If you jump out of the jeep and follow Gennaro,
turn to page 3.**

If you stay in the jeep, turn to page 48.

**If you just can't make up your mind,
turn to page 23.**

You get out of the jeep. Then you get back in. Then you get out again. All this time T-rex is thundering toward you!

You jump in again, and the snarling T-rex rocks the jeep back and forth. Then it lowers its head and peers inside. Its breath is even *more* disgusting than that lunch they served on the plane. You wish you could scream!

Paralyzed with fright, you think: *If only I live through this, I'll be a perfect kid forever! I'll cook! I'll take out the trash—without complaining! I'll do the dishes every night! Laundry? It's my specialty!*

Suddenly T-rex stands up. It takes a giant step toward the little shed where Mr. Gennaro is hiding.

You start breathing again. You didn't end up as a T-rex appetizer after all! Now the power flashes back on the computer screen and your jeep starts moving down the road. You're going to escape T-rex! You're going to live!

But you've got to keep your promise, which means you'll be busy doing housework for the rest of your life, from now all the way until . . .

THE END

You stay in the jeep. Tim runs toward the gentle giants. Mr. Hammond and Lex aren't far behind him. Now the three of them are standing at the edge of the moat, waiting for one of the dinosaurs to lean its head over to be petted.

Let them pet first, you think. *If they survive, maybe I'll give it a try*.

You notice another oddly-shaped hole in one of the fences. *That's funny*, you think. *I wonder if something escaped?* But you don't have time to wonder for long because suddenly one of the Brachiosaurs stretches its long neck way over the moat—right in your direction! You're face to face with a prehistoric monster! Yikes! Leaping out of the jeep, you take off, running at top speed, not looking or caring where you're going— which is why you don't see the log that trips you and sends you rolling down, down, down into a deep gorge. You keep rolling and rolling until you come to a stop at the bottom.

"Are you okay?" calls Lex, peering down from above.

Turn to page 25.

"I'm fine," you call back. Then you stand up and brush yourself off.

"I'll send help!" Mr. Hammond calls. "Just stay right where you are!"

As if you'd even *think* of wandering off! You sit down on a clump of giant tree roots to wait. You wait for what seems like a long time. When you get hungry, you nibble on a few purple berries growing near the tree roots. You really hope you won't have to wait much longer, because dark clouds are gathering in the sky. Suddenly, you hear a clap of thunder! At least you *hope* it's thunder—and not some "thunder lizard!"

Yep. It's thunder. You can tell because it's started to rain—hard! You're getting soaked. You scurry for a cluster of trees to keep dry when—OOMPH! You slip in the mud and bump into somebody. Then somebody grabs you—by the neck!

Quick! Pick a number between one and ten!

If you picked an even number, turn to page 26.

If you picked an odd number, turn to page 50—and good luck!

"Ulp!" you say.

"What are you doing here, kid?" says a gruff voice. "Spying on me?"

"N-n-n-no," you manage, and the grip loosens.

Standing before you is a mean-looking, heavy-set man in a yellow slicker. What's that he's holding? It looks like . . . a can of shaving cream?

"Well, you've seen me now," the man growls. "You can probably guess what I've got inside this shaving cream can."

"Uh . . ." You take a wild guess. "Shaving cream?"

The man laughs meanly and then says, "No! I'm smuggling out dinosaur embryos in the bottom of this can. There are fifteen specimens in here." He shakes the can at you. "I've got to get going," he continues. "There might be a Dilophosaur around here, and . . ." The big man stops mid-sentence.

Now, in the distance, you hear a spooky hooting sound.

The man looks around. "That's one now!" he says. "If one of those babies spits in your face, you'll . . ."

Turn to page 40.

For the next three hours, while Tim watches the movie, you and Lex chat—mostly about all the people Lex communicates with in cyberspace on her computer.

As you get off the plane, you see palm trees. You can hardly believe it—you're in South America! But before you have time to figure out which *country* in South America, you are whisked into a helicopter and whirled off to Isla Nublar, the mysterious island.

When the helicopter lands, you watch as Lex and Tim run into the arms of a man with a cane, who must be John Hammond. He looks about the same age as Gramma Dottie. He's wearing glasses and is dressed all in white. Even his beard and his hat are white.

"It's so good to see you kids!" says the man. And then, looking over at you, he winks. "It's good to see you, too. My, my, you look like Dottie!"

You think maybe this guy needs stronger glasses. At least you hope he does.

"Come on," says Mr. Hammond, ushering you and Lex and Tim to a nearby jeep that runs on a rail. "I can hardly wait to show you my park. I've spared no expense!"

Go to page **28.**

You all hop into the jeep and Mr. Hammond presses down on the accelerator. "I wouldn't let the others start the tour without you. After all, kids are our real audience!"

From the jeep, you see that the island is covered with thick green plants. It looks just like the jungles you've seen on *Nature*. Except for all the fences. There's a big hole in the fence beside a sign that says RAPTOR PIT. You wonder if it's supposed to be there.

But before you can ask Mr. Hammond about it, he screeches the jeep to a halt in front of a building that's still under construction. A sign says VISITORS' CENTER. But with bars on all the windows, you think it looks more like a jail. You follow him inside, where a group of people are standing around beside two huge half-built skeletons that could only be . . . dinosaurs?

"Kids, meet Dr. Alan Grant," Mr. Hammond says.

"The paleontologist?" asks Tim. "I read your book!"

Dr. Grant is backing away from Tim, but Tim just keeps talking. "Dr. Grant, do you really think that dinosaurs evolved into birds? But then how do you explain that birds have no teeth?"

If you want Dr. Grant to answer Tim's questions, go to page 33.

If you want Dr. Grant to keep backing away, go to page 38.

"Tim!" calls Mr. Hammond. "Tim! Are you all right?"

"I . . . I think so," comes Tim's voice from below.

"Okay!" Mr. Hammond yells down to him, and he starts pacing crazily back and forth along the edge of the moat. "Don't get excited! Don't get upset! And whatever you do, DON'T PANIC!"

"Don't worry, John!" a familiar voice calls up from the bottom of the moat. "I'll take care of Tim!"

You look down. There's Tim, and . . . can it be?

Turn to page 53.

"Hey!" you cry.

"It's Dr. Malcolm!" Mr. Hammond says.

As soon as everyone turns to look, Dr. Malcolm's head disappears from the little window. Slowly, the door creaks open, and Dr. Malcolm crawls out. He's got a wicked-looking gash on his forehead and his all-black clothes are ripped and shredded. But worst are his eyes—he's looking right at you—but does he see you?

"In the end," Dr. Malcolm whispers hoarsely, "everything is unpredictable!" With that, he collapses onto the floor.

You and Dr. Sattler and Dr. Grant run over to see if you can help him.

"This is a Raptor slash," Dr. Grant says as he examines the mathematician's head.

"I don't know, Alan," says Dr. Sattler as she looks at Dr. Malcolm's wound. "Maybe he just bumped his head on something."

"On something like a Raptor claw," insists Dr. Grant.

While Dr. Grant and Dr. Sattler argue about the gash, you perform CPR on Dr. Malcolm. Soon he's breathing again and his pulse is stabilized.

Dr. Malcolm opens his eyes, grasps your hand, and points a finger toward the kitchen door. "Life," he says, "always finds a way!"

Go to page 31.

You think he's thanking you. But when you look to where his finger is pointing you realize what he means. He means that *dinosaur life* has *found a way* to get into the kitchen! And now it's coming *out* of the kitchen—a trio of Raptors!

"Raptors!" you cry.

One of the Raptors is looking you right in the eye.

"Run for your life," you shriek.

"I think that's an *excellent* idea," Dr. Grant says, and he and Dr. Sattler zoom off faster than a couple of Olympic track stars.

They escape—just in the nick of time. Which is more than you, Tim, Lex, and Mr. Hammond do. Now you're stuck with poor Dr. Malcolm. The four of you manage to pull him into the kitchen and barricade the door with every piece of furniture you can find.

"We're safe in here," Mr. Hammond whispers.

If you agree with Mr. Hammond, turn to page 32.

If you think anyone who talks about "safety" when Raptors are on the prowl must be off his rocker, turn to page 45.

Mr. Hammond picks up the phone in the kitchen and dials the National Guard in a nearby South American country. They promise to be there within the hour.

One hour. You look at the kitchen door. The Raptors are pounding against your barricade. *BAM! BAM!* Your only hope is that the National Guard will hurry!

"Maybe we'd be more comfortable waiting inside the walk-in freezer," suggests Mr. Hammond, as the Raptors break through the doors.

You lead the way! Tim and Lex are close behind. Mr. Hammond just makes it in. He slams the door hard.

WHEW! That was a close one! There's no way they can break down the freezer door.

Boy, you never realized how really cold it is inside a deep freezer. You and Tim and Lex start doing jumping jacks to keep your blood moving. You only hope you won't turn into human popsicles before the National Guard arrives.

Hey! The door handle! It's turning! But—is it the National Guard? Or—have the Raptors figured out how to open the door?

Flip a coin!

Heads? Turn to page 34.

Tails? Turn to page 35.

"Well, a few species of dinosaur . . ." begins Dr. Grant.

"And this is Dr. Ellie Sattler," interrupts Mr. Hammond, waving an arm at a slim, blonde woman. "A paleobotanist."

Next, Mr. Hammond has you shake hands with Dr. Malcolm, mathematician, and with Mr. Gennaro, a lawyer, who's all decked out in a safari suit. Mr. Gennaro, you notice, looks very nervous.

And you're starting to feel nervous, too. Every time you turn around, somebody's talking about *dinosaurs!*

"Okay, everyone," Mr. Hammond says. "Go outside to the jeeps! The tour is about to begin!"

"But I'm hungry," says Lex. "I want something to eat first."

If you're hungry, too, turn to page 42.

If you're ready to start the tour, turn to page 8.

It's heads, and it's Raptors opening the freezer door! In they hop, with their claws out and their mouths wide open.

In a panic, you reach behind you on the freezer shelf, picking up a large, rock-hard package of frozen meat. You heave it at the Raptor closest to you. *WHACK!* It catches the Raptor right in the teeth!

"Good idea!" shouts Mr. Hammond. He and Tim and Lex begin hurling packages of frozen meat at the Raptors. Before you know it, all three are pawing at their jaws, trying to dislodge the frozen food!

Here's your chance! You run by them and out of the freezer, slamming the door behind you! The Raptors are trapped!

"To think," says Mr. Hammond, as you and Tim and Lex follow him back to the main room of the Visitors' Center, "our lives were saved by forty pounds of frozen chopped meat!"

"Yeah," you say, "it worked better than a *burger alarm!*"

Mr. Hammond has never heard such a horrible joke! Before you can tell another one, he calls a helicopter to take you off the island. Faster than you can say, "Fast food!" your adventure at Jurassic Park has come to . . .

THE END

Tails—the freezer door swings open and in walks a man in a general's uniform. Behind him you see several hundred soldiers. The best thing you see is—no Raptors!

Before you know it, you're sitting between Tim and Lex again, on a plane. This time you're headed back to America.

The flight attendant announces, "Ladies and gentlemen, the in-flight movie is about to begin."

Uh-oh! Do you have a funny feeling you've seen the movie before? Would you rather *die* than have to watch it again!

Yes? Then turn to page 56!

No? Then—quick! Turn to page 7!

"DR. SATTLER!" you cry. "RAAAAAAPTORS!"

She still doesn't hear you. But the helicopter pilot does! Suddenly the chopper descends. You do, too.

"Dr. Sattler!" you call again.

She looks up! She hears you—because you're about to swing right into her head! Instead of ducking out of the way, Dr. Sattler reaches up and grabs the rope just above your hands.

"Raptors!" you cry hoarsely.

There they are! Right in front of you! And there *you* are, dangling on the end of a rope like a piece of bait!

Just as their mouths open up, the pilot lifts the chopper up again. You skim over the heads of the vicious Raptors, and kick out. Got one—right on the chin!

"Nice work!" exclaims Dr. Sattler.

Before you know it, you're back at the Visitors' Center cafeteria, having a snack and listening to Dr. Sattler tell Mr. Hammond, Dr. Grant, Lex, and Tim how incredibly brave you are.

You're on top of the world. Suddenly you get the feeling somebody's watching you. You glance over at the swinging doors to the kitchen. A face is peering through the little glass window!

If you see a human face, turn to page 30.

If you see a Raptor's face, turn to page 37.

"RAPTORS!" you cry.

"Calm down—you're seeing things," advises Dr. Sattler. "It's over now."

With a shaky finger you point toward the doors.

"What?" Mr. Hammond says, getting up and walking to the kitchen.

"Don't!" you shout. "I know I saw a Raptor in there!"

Dr. Grant and Dr. Sattler follow Mr. Hammond into the kitchen.

"I'm going, too," says Tim.

"Wait for me," says Lex.

You put your head down on the table. Were you hallucinating?

Then all of a sudden, you hear a terrible crashing of metal pots and pans. People are shrieking! You've got to help them!

Grabbing the only weapon handy—the plastic knife from your tray—you run toward the kitchen door. But just at that second, someone—or some*thing*—is running *out* of the kitchen door, and

WHAP!

The door meets your face—hard! You're out cold.

Turn to page 52.

Dr. Grant backs into the door of the Visitors' Center. He turns, opens the door, and runs out into the jungle.

"I forgot!" Mr. Hammond says. "Dr. Grant thinks all kids are noisy, messy, and smelly."

"We are not!" you cry. "I'm going to prove it to him!" With that, you run out the door after Dr. Grant, yelling at the top of your lungs. As you run through the jungle, plants tear at your clothes and you fall down in the mud. Once you fall down in something that you *wish* had been mud!

"Dr. Grant!" you scream. "Kids are *not* all noisy, messy, and smelly!"

"*You* are," says Dr. Grant stepping out from behind a tree trunk, "but you are also very brave to come looking for me! Because of you, I've changed my mind about kids!"

Because of you, Dr. Grant marries and fathers six children. They are all noisy, messy, and oh, those diapers! But he doesn't care, because in an emotional moment out there in that jungle, you promised to baby-sit for his future children—for free! Bet you never thought this is how *this* story would come to . . .

THE END

You, Tim, and Lex hop out of the jeep and follow Mr. Hammond down to the large concrete moat. Boy, are those dinosaurs BIG! You feel about the size of an ant at a picnic.

Mr. Hammond extends his arm toward the big beasts and starts making funny little cooing noises. Lex and Tim look sort of embarrassed.

Suddenly, a Brachiosaur that had been munching on some treetops lowers its head and stretches its neck in your direction. Mr. Hammond gives its nose, which is about the size of a dining room table, a few pats. Tim reaches out to pet the dinosaur, too. But he reaches out too far and . . . oops!

"Help!" he cries as he slides down the moat.

Turn to page 29.

But before the fat man can finish his sentence, you hear another hoot behind you, and suddenly a big glob of tarry-looking goo lands smack in the middle of his forehead!

"AIIIIGH!" he screams. He drops the shaving cream can and begins to claw at his skin. "Help! My face is burning!" he cries. "My eyes! I can't see!"

You turn and see a weird-looking dinosaur peeking out from behind a tree. It has a long neck, a crest on its head, and a grin full of pointy teeth.

Hoot!

Pit-toohey! Another glob lands on the man's face.

As he writhes in agony, a pair of Dilophosaurs start hopping around him, hooting like crazy.

While the dinosaurs are hooting and hopping, you start hopping, too—away! Far away from the fat man who's not even yelling anymore. As you hop off into the pouring rain, your foot kicks the can of shaving cream and—what the heck—you pick it up and keep going.

Turn to page 41.

As you reach the road, Mr. Hammond shows up in a jeep and drives you safely back toward the Visitors' Center. On the way, you tell him about what happened to the fat man.

"Too bad," says Mr. Hammond. "That must have been Dennis Nedry, our computer expert. For some reason, he shut down our whole system and caused a lot of problems."

You hold up the can of shaving cream and tell Mr. Hammond what you know about it. He's so grateful to you for saving the dinosaur specimens that he gives you half of Isla Nublar. Half of Jurassic Park is yours!

You and Mr. Hammond open Jurassic Park together and it is wildly successful. Tim becomes the resident dinosaur expert and Lex, naturally, takes over Mr. Nedry's job as computer expert.

You are rich beyond imagination. You use some of your millions to fly Gramma Dottie and your parents over to visit you several times a year. As for finishing school—forget it! Dozens of colleges give you honorary degrees. You marry, have many children, live happily ever after until you die peacefully in your sleep at the age of 107, and that's . . .

THE END

"Catch up with us later!" shouts Mr. Hammond as he points you and Lex in the direction of the Visitors' Center cafeteria.

In the line, you pick out a burger.

"Yuck," says Lex as she selects a salad. "How can you eat animal flesh?"

After lunch, which you don't really enjoy that much after Lex's description of your food, Lex suggests that you look around before you meet the others.

"Okay," you say, and you follow her through a pair of shiny stainless-steel doors. You enter a laboratory lit with a strange glow. Lights are shining on dozens of eggs, keeping them warm.

"Look!" says Lex. "Some of the eggs are hatching!"

Sure enough, right in front of you, an egg is cracking open!

"It's a lizard!" you exclaim as a tiny yellow head with brown stripes peeks out of the egg.

Lex holds out her hand and the lizard scampers up her arm.

"Hey!" says a voice behind you. "Put that down!"

You turn and see a stern-faced man walking rapidly toward you.

"I'm Robert Muldoon, the game warden here," the man says. "And that's no lizard. It's a Raptor."

Turn to page 43.

"A Raptor!" exclaims Lex, swiping frantically at the creature that's now crawling on the back of her neck.

"What's a Raptor?" you say.

"A Velociraptor," says Mr. Muldoon, plucking the animal off Lex's neck and putting it back inside its egg shell. "I don't think Mr. Hammond should be breeding such dangerous dinosaurs."

"Dinosaurs?"

"Of course," mutters Mr. Muldoon, waving a hand at the incubating eggs all around the room. "What did you think was in Jurassic Park, puppy dogs?"

"Raptors are vicious killers!" exclaims Lex.

Mr. Muldoon nods. "They can run sixty miles an hour," he tells you. "And they've got claws like razor blades."

Turn to page 44.

"Excuse me, Mr. Muldoon," you say, "but are there any *full-grown* Raptors in Jurassic Park?"

"Of course," Mr. Muldoon replies. "But don't worry. They're all in the Raptor pit, surrounded by an electric fence."

Uh-oh. That hole you saw in the fence—wasn't it right by the Raptor pit?

As you tell Mr. Muldoon about it, his eyes grow wide with terror. He picks up a phone, dials the Control Center, and orders a complete evacuation of Jurassic Park.

Before you know it, you're in a helicopter with Mr. Muldoon, Lex, Tim, and Mr. Hammond, flying toward Miami.

"Well, the experiment is over," Mr. Muldoon says.

"Oh, uh, yes," mumbles Mr. Hammond.

You watch as Isla Nublar gets smaller and farther away.

"The dinosaurs on the island will live for a while, but soon they'll become extinct," Mr. Muldoon goes on. "And that will be the end of dinosaurs on earth."

Or . . . will it? Mr. Hammond's jacket opens for a moment and you catch a glimpse of two small yellow heads with brown stripes in his pocket! He's bringing Raptors into the U.S.A.! For life as we all know it, this is definitely . . .

THE END

You're right! Mr. Hammond is a few cards short of a full deck.

Behind the stainless-steel cabinets you catch a glimpse of a head—a head with scales!

You look around the room. "The only way out of here is up—through the air ducts!" you whisper.

You pick up a soup ladle and throw it to the other side of the kitchen. It lands with a clang. As the alert Raptor moves toward the noise, the four of you manage to climb up onto a high cabinet, pulling the unconscious Dr. Malcolm with you. Into the air duct you go, with the Raptor snapping at your heels.

You make slow progress, but at last you come out near the entrance to the Visitors' Center. If you can make it out to the helicopter pad, you think, you really *might* be safe.

"You kids go on," says Mr. Hammond. "I'll stay here with Dr. Malcolm. After all, I have to take responsibility for all of this."

"We'll send help," Tim promises.

You and Tim and Lex run out the door and head for the helicopters.

Go to page 47.

What are you, crazy? You're fifty feet in the air, being rescued from a dinosaur-infested jungle, and you let go of the rope?

Okay, okay, it's your story.

You fall fast—*THUD!* You land right in the Raptors' path, scaring them half to death! *WHISH!* They take off in a hurry just as Dr. Sattler comes along.

"What happened?" she gasps.

You are lying flat on your back. You've had the wind knocked out of you, so you can't say a word. And that's the *best* thing that happened to you on your fall.

Luckily, Dr. Sattler is an ace at first aid. She runs to her jeep, gets a board, straps you to it, and takes you back to the Visitors' Center. From there, you are evacuated by helicopter to the Hospital for Broken Bones and Lots of 'Em—which happens to be in St. Louis. There, a team of medical experts wheels you into surgery, and after only seventy-six operations, you're good as new.

"Well, almost," says Gramma Dottie, who comes to visit you every day.

You're not sure where it hurts the most. You hurt everywhere! That's why you're glad this story has come to . . .

THE END

The helicopter pad is just outside the gate. But the gate is shut. There's no way to open it!

"We'll have to scale the fence," says Lex.

"What about that?" you say, pointing to a sign that says: DANGER: 10,000 VOLTS.

"I know where the maintenance shed is," Tim says. "I can turn off the power from there. Come on!"

The three of you run to the shed, down the stairs, and along the hallway until you come to the control box. Tim starts flipping the little red switches from ON to OFF. Suddenly, you're in total darkness.

"Um . . . " you say. "Anybody bring a flashlight?"

Nobody did. You kids fumble around in that shed for nearly an hour trying to find the stairs. By the time you walk back out into the daylight, you're not the only ones who know that the fence isn't on anymore!

Every dinosaur in Jurassic Park is running loose!

"Back into the shed!" you cry.

You and Lex and Tim run in, slamming the door behind you.

"What should we do now?" Tim asks. "Turn the power back on?"

If you want to turn the power back on, turn to page 51.

If you want to leave the power off, turn to page 51.

You are too frozen with fear to move a muscle, so all you can do is watch as the T-rex bursts through the fence and comes roaring in your direction.

As you sit there, stiller than a statue, the terrible T-rex circles the jeep, bellowing and thrashing its tail. It's opening and closing its jaws.

You have only one thought in your head: After you are devoured by the dinosaur, boy, are your parents ever going to be sorry that they didn't get *you* a ticket to Hawaii!

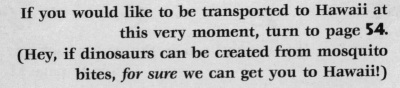

If you would like to be transported to Hawaii at this very moment, turn to page 54.
(Hey, if dinosaurs can be created from mosquito bites, *for sure* we can get you to Hawaii!)

Otherwise, just turn the page.

You close your eyes and wait for doom to strike.

"Don't eat me!" you cry.

You hope the pain will be over quickly. Already you can feel the T-rex brushing against your shoulder.

"Don't eat me!" you sob.

It's shaking your shoulder now, but . . . no teeth are ripping you apart. You open your eyes. It's dark. As your eyes adjust, you see a flight attendant standing over you, shaking your shoulder.

"You were having a nightmare," she whispers. "I told the captain we shouldn't show *The Day the Dinosaurs Took Over*, but does he ever listen to me?"

"Where am I?" you say.

"On your way to St. Louis, of course," she says. "We'll be landing in fifteen minutes." Then she pulls something from her pocket. Even in the semidarkness, you can see that it's that pair of gold plastic junior pilot wings. She pins them on to your T-shirt.

"Thanks," you mutter, as you look up at the movie screen just in time to see a pair of dinosaurs walking off into the sunset, and that's when you know that it's . . .

THE END

You try to yell, "Hey! Let go!" But all that comes out is "Caccckkkkk."

"Oh, I'm sorry!" The someone lets go. "You just took me by surprise."

You see a blonde woman holding a large syringe.

"I'm Dr. Sattler," she says. "I'm a paleobotanist. I do research with Dr. Grant, a paleontologist. I was just checking on a sick Triceratops. Come over here. I'll show you."

Forgetting all about waiting for help to arrive, you follow Dr. Sattler through the rain over to a clearing where a huge horned beast is lying on its side.

"I think she ate some poisonous berries," Dr. Sattler says, petting the Trike's head gently.

Poisonous berries? You're starting to feel sort of dizzy.

"Look," Dr. Sattler says, "her tongue is all purple."

Purple poisonous berries? Now you're getting a really bad feeling in your stomach.

Do you think *you* ate poisonous berries? Quick! Call the poison-control hot line! Then, while you're waiting for the ambulance to arrive, turn to page 16.

Do you think the berries you ate were harmless prehistoric purple berries? Turn to page 5.

Let's face it—it doesn't matter *what* you do. If you turn the power back on, you can't scale the fence without being electrocuted. If you leave the power off, you're stuck inside that shed.

Unless . . . Is that thunder you hear? And what's that banging noise?

Look! Something's kicking at the side of the shed! A scaly foot is coming through! There's another foot! Now a Tyrannosaurus rex is prying the shed open like a big, prehistoric can opener! It's knocking off the roof and . . . Do you really want all the gory details? Or shall we just say that this story has come to a . . .

DEAD END

You open you eyes. It's very quiet. Your head hurts and you're really hungry. But where *are* you? You're lying on the floor. And it sure doesn't look like the floor of Gramma Dottie's apartment. Then you remember. Jurassic Park! Raptors in the kitchen!

Slowly you get to your feet. Your head is throbbing! You peek into the kitchen. It's a mess, but no one's there. But look, on the floor. Isn't that Lex's little computer game? And next to that is Tim's precious book on dinosaurs!

The bad feeling in your stomach gets worse when you glance out the window. Raptors are running everywhere! And there's a T-rex chasing after them! Dinosaurs have taken over! You realize now that you're the only human left alive on Isla Nublar!

GRRRRRR!

What was *that*? Could it be your stomach growling? You wish! As you walk into the kitchen you hear the sound of sharp nails scratching a highly polished floor. The sound is getting closer and closer and, sorry to say, so is . . .

THE END

"Gramma Dottie?" you call down. "Is that *you?*"

"In the flesh! Thought I'd surprise you!" she calls up. "Darned helicopter missed the landing pad coming in and I ended up down here."

"Dorothy!" calls Mr. Hammond. "This *is* a surprise."

He jogs back to his jeep, gets a rope, and ten minutes later, Tim and Gramma Dottie are standing beside you.

Gramma Dottie gives you a big hug and then turns to Mr. Hammond. "Dinosaurs, John!" she exclaims. "I should have known you'd come up with an idea for a theme park that was better than some little cartoon rodent."

Mr. Hammond is beaming. He takes Gramma Dottie's hand. "Come, Dorothy, my dear," he says. "Let me give you a personal tour of Isla Nublar and Jurassic Park. Let me assure you, I've spared no expense."

Turn to page 55.

Aloha! Welcome to Waikiki Beach! Take a deep breath and smell that fresh sea breeze! Take a look around. Palm trees! White sand! And best of all, surf's up!

You grab one of the surfboards stacked up by the water's edge and head out to catch the big one. You're kneeling on the board, paddling out beyond the surf with your hands. You made it! Now you're kneeling on your board waiting for the perfect wave.

And—is this it?

You look behind you and see a giant swell of water headed your way. It's the big one, all right. You start paddling with all your might to catch that wave!

But—what are those funny-looking things sticking out of the water? Could they be . . . fins? You got it! You're surfing right in the middle of a school of sharks!

You thought you were paddling fast before, but that was nothing compared to the speed you're traveling now! Quick! Stand up on that board! That's the way! And you'd better keep standing up because if you fall, those funny little fins circling around you will definitely spell out . . .

THE END!

Hand in hand, your grandmother and Tim and Lex's grandfather walk off down the road.

"But Grandpa!" cries Tim. "I thought you were going to give *us* a tour!"

"You kids take the jeep," Mr. Hammond says, not even bothering to turn around. "The interactive CD-ROM will tell you everything you want to know about Jurassic Park."

You and Tim and Lex head for the jeep. As it takes off down the road, you pass Mr. Hammond and Gramma Dottie. You wave, but they're too busy talking to notice. You have a feeling that for those two this is just the beginning.

But not so for you and Tim and Lex. From the moment Lex spots another hole in the fence by the Raptor pit and you start hearing strange noises, you have a bad feeling in the pit of your stomach—because right around the next corner might be . . .

THE END

You hear a funny sputtering sound coming from the plane's engine.

"Oh, no!" cries Tim, pointing out the window. "There's smoke coming from the wing!"

Now the little oxygen masks drop from the little trapdoor in the ceiling. As you strap one over your face, you can feel how fast the plane is falling. Here you are—snatched from the jaws of dinosaurs only to perish in a horrible disaster!

Too bad! What a really icky way for this story to come to . . .

THE END!

Don't Miss These Other Exciting
Jurassic Park Books

Jurassic Park
The Movie Storybook

Jurassic Park
The Junior Novelization

The Dinosaurs of Jurassic Park
An easy-to-read book

Raptor Attack
With a 3-D poster and glasses